To my son, Franek

Designed by Monika Keano

Published simultaneously in Canada by HarperCollins*CanadaLtd*

Printed and bound in the United States of America

Library of Congress catalog card number: 95-44018

First edition, 1996

Tomek Bogacki

Cat and Mouse

Frances Foster Books

Farrar Straus Giroux

NEW YORK

Mother Mouse was teaching her children about the world . . . But not all of them. One little mouse was not paying attention. She was curious about everything.

Mother Cat was teaching her children about the world, too. But one little cat was not paying attention. He was curious, too.

The curious little mouse and the curious
little cat met in the green meadow.

"I have never seen an animal so different
from me," said the mouse.

"*I* have never seen an animal so different from *me*," said the cat.

The little mouse made a terrifying face.
"Are you afraid of me?" she asked.
"No!" said the cat.

The little cat made himself as big and
as scary as he could.
"Are you afraid of *me*?" he asked.
"No!" said the mouse.

So the little mouse and the little cat began to play.

They rolled down the hill.

They swung from a tree.

They played and played . . .

. . . until the sun went down.

"Come home, come home, little mouse,"
called Mother Mouse. "It is getting dark."

"Come home, come home, little cat,"
called Mother Cat. "It is getting late."

"I have never had so much fun!" the little mouse said to her sisters.
"I played with a cat!"
"How could you have fun with a cat?" they asked.

"I made friends with a mouse," the little cat
said to his brothers.
"I have never had so much fun."
"How could you be friends with a mouse?"
they asked.

Then the other little mice and the other little
cats got curious, too. The very next day they
all met in the green meadow . . .